RICHARD SCARRY'S
Great Big Schoolhouse
Readers

Get That Hat!

Illustrated by Huck Scarry
Written by Erica Farber

STERLING CHILDREN'S BOOKS
New York

Lowly has a hat.
Lowly likes that hat.

2

The wind likes that hat, too.
WHOOSH!

The wind blows.
The hat blows away.

Oh, no!
Get that hat!

5

The hat is in a tree.

It is up, up, up.

A bird is in the tree.

It is up, up, up.

Huckle goes up, up, up.

TWEET! TWEET!
The bird flies away.
The hat flies away, too.

8

Oh, no!

Get that hat!

Huckle and Lowly go, go, go.

Bridget and Arthur go, go, go.

The bird and the hat go, go, go.

The hat falls.

It falls on a car.

The car goes.

Oh, no!

Get that hat!

The car goes fast.

The hat goes fast.

The car stops.

The hat falls!

It falls in the mud.

Huckle and Lowly run.
Bridget and Arthur run.

Too late!
Up goes the mud.
Up goes the hat.

Down goes the mud.

SPLAT!

There goes that hat!

Up go Huckle and Lowly.

Up go Arthur and Bridget.

WHOOSH goes the wind!
There goes that hat!

The hat falls.

It falls on a head.

It is not Lowly's head.

It is Molly's head.

Silly hat!

Lowly puts on the hat.
Lowly likes that hat.

The wind likes that hat, too.

The wind blows.

The hat blows away.

Oh, no! Get that hat!

STERLING CHILDREN'S BOOKS
New York

An Imprint of Sterling Publishing
387 Park Avenue South
New York, NY 10016

ISBN 978-1-4027-9918-1 (hardcover)
ISBN 978-1-4027-9919-8 (paperback)

Produced by

 JR Sansevere

Distributed in Canada by Sterling Publishing
℅ Canadian Manda Group, 165 Dufferin Street
Toronto, Ontario, Canada M6K 3H6
Distributed in the United Kingdom by GMC Distribution Services
Castle Place, 166 High Street, Lewes, East Sussex, England BN7 1XU
Distributed in Australia by Capricorn Link (Australia) Pty. Ltd.
P.O. Box 704, Windsor, NSW 2756, Australia

For information about custom editions, special sales, premium and corporate purchases,
please contact Sterling Special Sales at 800-805-5489 or specialsales@sterlingpublishing.com.

Manufactured in China

Lot #:
2 4 6 8 10 9 7 5 3 1
11/14

www.sterlingpublishing.com/kids

24